CW00957550

Rupert Dumbleton

Lucy and Lupin and the Kidnappers

With help from
Janet Bloye, Eileen Simmonds and Dorothy Williams
2018

11E

Angela Cummings

Lucy woke up, looked first at the ceiling then across her bedroom to find Lupin sleeping quietly on his mat by the window with his nose between his paws. Lupin was such a light sleeper that she had never been able to get anywhere near him before he woke up so she decided to throw a pillow at him instead. As quietly as she could, she raised herself in bed and carefully lifted the pillow above her head and took aim only to find that Lupin was already sitting up and watching her with a curious expression on his face. He easily dodged the pillow then prepared himself for the mock fight which was their usual form of greeting in the morning.

With the formalities over, Lucy tiptoed over to the bedroom door and listened for any sound below which would indicate that her mother was up and about. A clank of crockery suggested that breakfast was being prepared so Lucy climbed down the stairs and into the kitchen with Lupin trailing behind her.

"Hello mum have I got to go to school today?"

"*Good morning mother and how are you today?*" corrected Mrs Wilson.

"Yes mum, good morning mum and have I got to go to school today?" said Lucy as she climbed up onto a stool by the kitchen table. Lucy knew that the half term holiday was approaching but did not know exactly when it was due.

Lupin ran over to greet Mrs Wilson but was told not to be silly.

"Do you know a girl called Angela Cummings?" asked Mrs Wilson as she set out the breakfast things.

"Yes," said Lucy as she shook cornflakes from a packet into her bowl, "she's the only one I like in my class. The others are all silly."

"According to the news she was kidnapped on the way home from school yesterday afternoon." said Mrs Wilson.

Lucy looked up from her cornflakes and asked what kidnapped meant.

"It's when somebody is taken prisoner and held in a secret place until somebody else pays a lot of money to get them released." explained Mrs Wilson.

"Her dad's got pots of money," said Lucy pouring milk onto her cornflakes, "so she'll be OK."

"I'm not so sure Lucy. We don't know where she is or what sort of people are holding her captive. It's not the sort of thing you expect to happen in a quiet little village like Witchwood. From now on you won't be able to go anywhere without an escort and I suppose the school will be closed until the police have completed their investigations."

"Oh good," said Lucy through a mouthful of cornflakes, "I don't like going to school."

"You don't seem to care what happens to your friend Angela as long as you can get out of going to school," said Mrs Wilson as she loaded two slices of bread into the toaster.

Lucy put down her spoon and looked up, "I like Angela but I don't know what to do about being kidnapped so I think I'll ask Mr

Pemberton. I bet he can find her"

"Half of the policemen in Warwickshire are already searching for Angela." said Mrs Wilson as she poured a cup of tea for herself, "However clever Mr Pemberton is I cannot see how he could possibly do better than a thousand policemen."

Lucy looked up and smiled.

Mr Pemberton was the retired gentleman who lived next door to the Wilsons. He had recently sold his chemists shop in Witchwood and now spent an hour or so every day preparing potions for some of his old customers who preferred their medicines to be prepared in the traditional way. When he had done that, he spent his time either attending to his large garden or, with the help of his old friend Mr Wilberforce, investigating any unsolved crime that happened to come to their attention. Lucy spent hours leaning on the garden fence and talking to Mr Pemberton about the trees in his garden, the clouds in the sky or anything else that occurred to her. He seemed to know everything and answered all of her questions patiently in a way that she could understand. She seemed to learn more from him than she did from school.

"When you have had your breakfast and washed and dressed, Lucy, we will go and find out whether the school is open." said Mrs Wilson looking sternly at Lucy and daring her to say something.

Lucy pulled a face but said nothing.

Twenty minutes later, when Lupin had been fed and Lucy had finished her breakfast and made herself ready, the three of them set out for Witchwood Junior School. Although besieged by the press, the headmistress was determined to keep the school open for the last full day of the term and made sure that the pupils were whisked quickly away to their classrooms. Lucy said goodbye to Lupin then followed the last of the stragglers into the school. Mrs Wilson comforted Lupin, who didn't like being separated from Lucy, then turned back along the high street to collect a few things from the shops before returning home.

In the shops the kidnapping was the sole topic of conversation. Mrs Wilson heard that Mr Cummings had made millions of pounds from the entertainment industry and now lived with his wife and only daughter in a huge house in a small but exclusive new development at the far end of Witchwood. No one seemed to know who the kidnappers were or what they had demanded in the way of a ransom.

Later that afternoon when Mrs Wilson was pegging washing on the line in her rear garden, she heard a gentle cough and turned to find the tall stooping figure of Mr Pemberton standing behind the fence near to the millstone on which Lucy stood when they held their long conversations.

"I apologise for interrupting you when you have work to do," began Mr Pemberton, "but I have just heard the news about the kidnapping at Lucy's school and wondered how you were coping with the situation."

"Well," said Mrs Wilson placing the basket of washing down on the millstone, "I find the idea that we have such evil people wandering the streets of Witchwood deeply disturbing but Lucy, although she regards Angela Cummings as her closest friend at school, doesn't seem to be at all concerned. She seems to think that either Mr Cummings will simply pay up and Angela will be freed straight away or, for some reason best known to herself, thinks that you will find and release the girl before the police manage to track her down."

"Hmm," said Mr Pemberton, "I do enjoy talking to Lucy, but I can't always follow her reasoning." He paused for thought then continued, "I suppose it's possible that the matter could have been resolved quickly and quietly by the payment of a large ransom but, now that the police are involved, the matter may become more complicated."

Again he paused for thought then continued, "I could have a word with Mr Wilberforce who has contacts within the police force and has more experience of criminal activity than I do. There may be something we can do to help to retrieve Angela but obviously we cannot match either the resources or the experience of the Warwickshire Police Force in such matters. Leave it with me, I will let you know what we find out."

With that Mr Pemberton bade Mrs Wilson farewell and ambled back into his house to telephone Mr Wilberforce. Mrs Wilson pegged out the remainder of the washing then put Lupin on his lead and went to collect Lucy from school.

Normally, children who lived in the same part of the village walked at least part of the way home in a small group so that they could look after each other. Now the pavement outside the school was crowded by parents anxious to make sure that their child would get home safely. Lucy was smaller than most of the children at the school and so it was difficult for Mrs Wilson to pick her out in the crowd that emerged from the school doorway and stampeded across the playground towards the school gate. At last Mrs Wilson caught a glimpse of blonde pigtails in the confusion and moved forwards to stop her from stooping down to cuddle Lupin amongst a surging mob of children and parents. Holding Lucy with one hand and Lupin's lead with the other, Mrs Wilson barged her way through the crowd then between the unusually large number of cars parked outside the school and across the high street to the comparative safety of the far pavement where dog and daughter were finally allowed to greet each other.

On their way home Mrs Wilson told Lucy of her conversation with Mr Pemberton and explained that he would let her know as soon as possible in what way, if any, he and Mr Wilberforce might be able to assist the police in the recovery of Angela Cummings.

"I knew he would help." said Lucy smiling happily.

When they reached home, Mrs Wilson told Lucy and Lupin to go and play in the garden while she prepared tea.

Lucy ran and climbed onto the millstone to see whether Mr Pemberton was in his garden but he was not there. Her disappointment lasted for several seconds until she noticed that Lupin had found their football under a laurel bush. There followed a very noisy game of one-side football which developed into a wrestling match ending only when Mrs Wilson called them in for tea.

"Why, as a matter of interest," said Mrs Wilson as Lucy tucked into beans on toast, "do you dislike everyone in your class except

Angela Cummings?"

"The other children don't like her because she's posh and they don't like me because I'd rather talk to grown ups who know things rather than children who don't know anything, so we stick together."

That, thought Mrs Wilson, not only explained why Lucy had so few friends of her own age but also why she spent so much time talking to Mr Pemberton.

"Good answer." said Mrs Wilson quietly to herself.

At half past six, Mrs Wilson turned on the television to catch the early evening news while Lucy sat on the floor and did a small wooden jigsaw puzzle on the coffee table. Despite the fact that the police had allocated huge resources to the search for Angela it would appear that they had made little progress and were now appealing for anyone who had witnessed any unusual activity anywhere in the area to contact them immediately.

At about quarter to seven Lucy declared that some of the pieces in the jigsaw didn't fit whichever way she tried them and decided to go to bed. Lupin woke instantly from his snooze beside the settee and trailed behind her. Mrs Wilson wished her goodnight and waited a few seconds for a reply that never came, then finished the jigsaw puzzle and left it for Lucy to find in the morning.

Half Term

When Lucy woke up the sun was shining through a gap in the bedroom curtains and Lupin was asleep on his mat by the window. Then she remembered that school would finish early that day and lay for few minutes smiling happily to herself. Eventually she climbed out of bed and took a step towards Lupin who awoke instantaneously and was ready to defend himself from the usual playful attack by Lucy. Instead she simply knelt down beside him and gave him a cuddle. Lupin was wary of Lucy's new tactic and stayed on guard.

All was right in Lucy's world except for the fact that her father was working in Scotland and that Angela had probably spent the night tied to a chair in a dark cellar. Lucy couldn't think of anything she could do to help

Angela so decided to talk to Mr Pemberton about the problem as soon as she got home from school.

In the kitchen Lucy greeted her mother with a cheerful good-morning-how-are-you-today and gave her a hug for good measure. Mrs Wilson was almost as surprised as Lupin had been by Lucy's change of mood.

"Good morning Lucy," replied Mrs Wilson, "I suppose you're happy because school finishes today."

"Yes and because we can start to rescue Angela."

"Mr Pemberton said only that he would talk the matter over with his friend Mr Wilberforce and let me know later today what they had been able to find out about the kidnapping. He said he would do whatever he could to help to find Angela but he did not promise to rescue her."

"Well I think he will." said Lucy confidently as she concocted a bowl of pink slush from cornflakes and blackcurrant juice.

Mrs Wilson delivered Lucy to school at nine o'clock and went to pick her up again at one o'clock in the afternoon. Just as they were finishing their lunch in the kitchen the front doorbell rang and Mrs Wilson invited Mr Pemberton into the house. He had barely finished his apology for interrupting her when Lucy ran up to him, grabbed his hand and pulled him into the hall. Lupin ran between their legs doing his best waggle dance until Mrs Wilson told them both to leave the poor man alone. She escorted Mr Pemberton into the living room, invited him to sit down and asked him whether he would like a cup of tea. Mr Pemberton never refused a cup of tea.

When Lucy and Lupin had calmed down, and with a cup of tea at his elbow, Mr Pemberton began to explain what he and Mr Wilberforce had discovered so far.

"When Angela failed to return home at the normal time on Wednesday afternoon," began Mr Pemberton, "her mother telephoned the school and was told that she had left with a group of other children about half an hour earlier. Mrs Cummings then walked along the route that her daughter normally took on her way back from school but failed to find her so reported the matter to the police who arrived at her house within minutes. The police immediately put out a general alert with a description of Angela and set about looking for witnesses to what they thought might be an abduction. From a list of the children who had walked part of the way with Angela the police quickly established where she had last been seen."

"The police then interviewed the occupants of houses in the in the immediate neighbourhood. Most of the houses within the new development were set back some distance from the road so the interviewers were not at all surprised to find that none of the residents had witnessed the abduction or seen or heard any unusual activity in the area. Several of the houses were unoccupied. Some of those were kept in respectable condition by occasional visits by window cleaners or gardeners. Others were simply locked and abandoned for the winter months.

"None of the people interviewed in the area could recollect seeing a person or vehicle of any description entering or leaving the development in the vital few minutes between the time that Angela was last seen and the arrival of the police. Angela seemed to have vanished into thin air.

"Members of the search team were still comparing notes at five o'clock when, Mr Cummings, who had been summoned by his wife from his office in Birmingham, arrived in his Mercedes and screeched to a halt between the police cars that were already parked in the driveway. He stormed into the house but, before the waiting police officers could question him, received a short call on his mobile phone from a man claiming to be one of the kidnappers. The caller said only that he would contact him again at eight o'clock in the morning to give him time to consider how much he valued his daughter's life then rang off. Mr Cummings fell silent then turned to face everyone in the room and told them, in a voice trembling with anger, that he had just been told that his daughter had been kidnapped. His wife collapsed in tears but, rather than comfort her, Mr Cummings began to pace up and down the room explaining in graphic detail what he would do to the kidnappers when he caught them. As soon as he had recovered his composure the police asked him whether he would allow them to release a photograph of Angela to newspapers and television channels in the hope that someone had seen her since she was abducted. Mr Cummings grunted his agreement and that, I think, resulted in the news bulletin that you saw on the mid evening news."

Mrs Wilson nodded.

Mr Pemberton continued, "In the absence of witnesses, the police brought in additional resources and began to widen their search. They also made arrangements to record any further telephone calls that Mr Cummings might receive on either the land line to the house or his mobile phone."

Lucy lost interest in the long explanation and wandered off to play with Lupin, but since Mrs Wilson seemed to be following his explanation, Mr Pemberton continued.

"At exactly eight o'clock this morning, the caller phoned again instructing Mr Cummings to take his mobile phone, some paper and a pencil to his car and set off immediately in the direction of Claverdon. The caller told him that he would receive details of the route that he was to take as soon as he was on the road. The caller warned him that any delay in carrying out this instruction or any attempt to follow him would have dire consequences for his daughter. With very bad grace and some terrible language, Mr Cummings picked up the items that had been requested, climbed into his Mercedes and reversed back out of his driveway with a squeal of tyres.

"Before Mr Cummings had reached Claverdon the caller rang to tell him to pull to the side or the road and take down details of the route he was to follow. The caller gave him a list of six public houses he was to drive past on a long circular route through central Warwickshire. He was instructed to drive steadily at a speed not exceeding forty miles an hour and to continue driving around the circuit until the kidnappers were sure that he was alone in the car and was not being followed. Then, and only then, he would be contacted and given instructions about the size of the ransom and how it was to be made. The caller told him that his daughter would not be released until twenty four hours after the ransom had been paid in accordance with the instructions he would be given. With that the caller rang off.

"From his car Mr Cummings phoned his wife, repeated the instructions that he had been given by the caller then rang off so that he could concentrate on the route that he been instructed to follow. After driving around the circuit for over an hour and a half, Mr Cummings received a call from the man who claimed to be one of the kidnappers to say that the deal was off because his car was being followed by a police helicopter. Mr Cummings, in the foulest of tempers, drove directly to his house in Witchwood and accused the police of risking his daughter's life by failing to carry out the kidnappers' instructions and then in a fit of rage he picked up a rather expensive vase and smashed it through a glass topped table. The senior officer present immediately apologised for their mistake and agreed not to make any further attempt to follow his car or to interfere in any arrangement he made with the kidnappers unless Mr Cummings requested them to do so. That seemed to calm him down but it left the police with the impression that Mr Cummings was a dangerously unpredictable man.

"That, according to Mr Wilberforce's contact in the police force, was the situation at nine o'clock last night. We understand that the search has since been widened with roadblocks at key locations but that no further sighting of Angela has been reported. Mr Wilberforce is at present updating our records and we intend to spend the remainder of the afternoon studying the information we have in greater detail in the hope that we can find a clue as to where Angela is being held."

With that Mr Pemberton finished his cup of tea, stood up and begged to be excused. Mrs Wilson, thanked him for giving her such a thorough explanation of recent developments, wished him the best of luck with his continuing investigation and showed him to the door.

Lucy who had been tickling Lupin's ear for the last few minutes realised that Mr Pemberton was about to leave and pleaded to go with him. Mrs Wilson explained to her that that the two gentlemen were going to be very busy and that they might not be able to concentrate on their work if they were distracted by a young girl and a small dog.

"On the contrary," said Mr Pemberton, "Lucy is one of the few people who knows both Angela Cummings and Witchwood Junior School, so may be in a position to help us with our investigation. Lupin may not be of use to us today, but as one of the finest tracker dogs I have ever met, he may be able to help us to track down Angela when we have a better idea of where to look for her."

With some reluctance, and having warned Lucy to be on her best behaviour at all times, Mrs Wilson decided that it was just possible that Lucy and Lupin might be of some assistance to the two old gentlemen in what seemed to be a fairly hopeless venture.

Lucy jumped up and shouted, "Yes." then ran around excitedly with Lupin at her heals.

Mrs Wilson watched the oddly matched group of investigators troop into Mr Pemberton's house, shook her head in disbelief, then turned to get on with her work.

The Yellow Route

Lucy took Lupin off his lead and followed Mr Pemberton along the hallway and into his large living room. Lucy had been there several times before but stood for a moment in the doorway gazing at the strange assortment of furniture, scientific equipment and other objects stacked, seemingly at random, in every available space. Against one wall stood a tall cabinet with dozens of identical drawers each carefully marked with abbreviated words which Lucy did not understand. Near to the opposite wall was a large mahogany table on which stood what looked to Lucy like a complicated chemistry set. Filling most of the far wall was a huge bookcase packed with books of all shapes, colours and sizes. By a large window overlooking the garden was a roll top desk overflowing with scrolls and paperwork. Next to it Mr Wilberforce sat in front of a computer at the far end of a trestle table on which a large map of Warwickshire was laid out.

As they approached the table Mr Wilberforce, dressed as always in a cream coloured suit, stood up to greet them. Lupin ran to him and performed one of his best waggle dances and was rewarded with a pat on the head for his trouble. Lucy didn't know what to do so she made a little curtsy. Mr Pemberton explained to Mr Wilberforce that Mrs Wilson had given permission for Lucy and Lupin to help them in their investigation into the kidnapping of Angela Cummings.

"Splendid," said Mr Wilberforce, "I understand that Lucy knows Angela as well as anyone at Witchwood Junior School and may indeed be able to help us understand the circumstances surrounding her disappearance."

Lupin ran off to investigate every thing in the room. Mr Wilberforce found an extra chair for Lucy and invited her to sit at the table. Mr Wilberforce, who was much more methodical than Mr Pemberton, opened a notebook entitled 'The Kidnapping of Angela Cummings', turned to a new page, took the cap off his fountain pen and looked up at the other members of the committee.

"I thought we might start the investigation," began Mr Wilberforce, "by discussing the reason why Angela Cummings might have been chosen as a kidnap victim."

He waited for a response.

"I think they napped Angela because her dad's got lots of money." volunteered Lucy.

"Good point." said Mr Wilberforce entering Lucy's suggestion in the notebook then asked whether they had any other ideas.

"Perhaps," suggested Mr Pemberton, "one of the kidnappers is a business rival, employee or someone else who bears a grievance against Mr Cummings and is seeking revenge.

"Money or revenge," said Mr Wilberforce to himself as he made another entry in his book.

"Now we turn to method." said Mr Wilberforce, drawing their attention to a map of central Warwickshire which lay open on the table, "You will see from the map that I have highlighted the location of the Cummings' house in red and marked the route that Mr Cummings had been instructed to follow in yellow. You will notice that the yellow route uses both main and minor roads and crosses the M40 motorway at Junctions 15 and 16. Most of the route is through open countryside but it also passes key points in built up areas."

Lucy got bored with discussion, slipped quietly off her chair and went to look for Lupin.

"Why," asked Mr Wilberforce, "do you think the kidnappers devised such an elaborate route for Mr Cummings to follow?"

"I can only think," said Mr Pemberton, "that they chose such a route because it would be almost impossible for a police car, or any other vehicle, to follow Mr Cummings for such a distance and through so many changes of direction without being detected. The fact that the kidnappers spotted the helicopter shows that a least one person was watching the route. If nothing else, it shows how careful and well organised the kidnappers are."

Mr Wilberforce made a few more notes

in his book then announced that the next and last item on his agenda was how, from the limited amount of information available to them, they could discover either where the kidnappers operated from or where the kidnap victim was being held.

Mr Pemberton considered the matter for a few minutes then suggested that they assume, as a starting point, that the kidnappers operated from close to or within the yellow circuit that Mr Wilberforce had marked on the map. Mr Wilberforce turned his attention to the map, assumed that the kidnappers operated from a point no further than five miles outside the yellow line and, using a scale rule and a calculator, estimated that the total area under consideration could be in the region of a hundred square miles. Much too large for the Warwickshire Police Force to search thoroughly in the time available and well beyond the capability of their own small team.

As the scale of the problem seemed to grow, Mr Wilberforce's confidence in their ability to solve it began to wane. After spending the best part of two days gathering and reviewing all of the information they could find, they still had no idea who had kidnapped Angela or where she was being kept.

"Cheer up Mr Wilberforce," said Mr Pemberton, "The more information we have at the beginning, the better chance we have of arriving at the correct solution at the end. I suggest that we spend the evening thinking about the problem and meet again tomorrow morning at say nine o'clock by which time your contact in the police force may be able to provide us with additional information."

With that Mr Pemberton went to search for Lucy and found her sitting under the big mahogany table talking to Lupin.

"Mr Wilberforce and I have finished our discussion for the time being Lucy. I'm sorry if you found it boring but we have to examine all of the evidence that we have so that we can plan what to do next."

"Do you know where Angela is yet?" asked Lucy as she crawled from under the table.

"Not yet," admitted Mr Pemberton "but with a bit of luck we may have a better idea of where she's being held by tomorrow. Now its time for you to go home before your mother starts to worry about you."

Mr Pemberton escorted Lucy and Lupin to the door and watched as she turned to wave to him as she disappeared into her own house.

"Now," said Mr Pemberton, "I think it's time to have another cup of tea and watch the early evening news to see whether the police have made any more progress in the search for Angela Cummings.

Mrs Wilson closed her eyes and grimaced as Lucy crashed into the hall and wanted to know when her father was coming home. Lucy loved her father but could not understand why he always seemed to be somewhere else.

"I'm sorry Lucy but your father is under a lot of pressure to complete the first phase of the hospital development in Scotland so that it can be opened officially by the Minister of Health on Monday morning. Because of that he may not be home until very late on Sunday or even Monday morning. He sends you his love and is looking forward to spending a few days with you next week."

"It's always next week." said Lucy and burst into tears. Her mother went to comfort her, wiped her tears away and asked whether she would like something special for tea. What she really wanted was for her father to come home but with a little persuasion she settled for alphabet spaghetti followed by vanilla ice cream with chocolate bits in it.

While she was having her tea, Mrs Wilson told Lucy that her Aunt Katherine had telephoned her to ask her whether she would like to go out with her the following day. Lucy liked her Aunt Katherine because she seemed to understand Lupin and always found something interesting for them to do. Lucy's mood changed slowly from despair to hope.

Tardebigge

When Lucy woke up the next morning she noticed Lupin standing by the bedroom door and listening to the sounds coming from below. After a few seconds he decided that it was only Mrs Wilson moving about in the kitchen so wandered back to his mat by the window and threw himself down again. Lucy knew that if there had been an unusual sound or movement below he would have made a series of little grunting sounds and looked anxiously at the crack between the door and the jamb to show her that he wanted to go to investigate. She climbed out of bed and was greeted by Lupin with a little waggle dance. She knelt down beside and gave him a cuddle then opened the bedroom door and they went down to the kitchen together.

"Good morning Mum. What am I doing today?"

"Good morning Lucy," replied her mother, "Aunt Katherine is coming to take you out, so when you've eaten your breakfast you have to get ready to go out. Remember it might be cold and wet today so put on some warm clothes and take your umbrella."

"Yes mum." said Lucy as she mixed cornflakes and rice krispies with milk and blackcurrant juice in her breakfast bowl, and stirred it into a lumpy pink mess onto which she sprinkled sugar. Mrs Wilson shook her head despairingly.

A few minutes later Katherine arrived and was greeted by her sister and Lupin in the hall. Lucy, through a mouthful of toast, shouted a muffled greeting from the kitchen. Her mother told her not to talk with her mouth full and ordered her to finish her breakfast and get ready to go out as soon as possible.

"She doesn't get any better does she." said Katherine with a broad smile as the two sisters retired to the living room to exchange the latest family news.

Eventually Lucy appeared wearing a winter coat, a woollen bobble hat and pink wellington boots. Lupin ran about excitedly. Mrs Wilson tidied Lucy up, checked that she had her gloves then shooed all three of them out of the front door and into Katherine's battered old estate car. Katherine checked that Lucy was strapped in then started the engine and, after some waving of hands, they were on their way.

Lucy wanted to know where they were going. Katherine told her that they were going to Tardebigge to look at a flight of locks. Lucy had never heard of Tardebigge and had forgotten what locks were.

"Do you remember walking along the canal at Stratford-upon-Avon and watching the boat rise up in that narrow channel between the two big wooden gates." said her aunt.

"Yes I remember now. The lady wound the handle and the boat came up."

Obviously Lucy hadn't grasped the principle of how locks worked but Katherine could put that right when they got to their destination.

"At Stratford you saw only two locks," said Katherine, "At Tardebigge there are thirty locks in a row and a big lake."

Lucy regarded anywhere she hadn't been before as an adventure. Tardebigge sounded particularly interesting because she knew Lupin liked anywhere there was mud and water.

"How far is it?"

"About twenty miles."

"How long will that take?"

"About half an hour."

And so the conversation went on until they ran into a queue of traffic and were told to pull into a lay-by by a policeman wearing a fluorescent yellow jacket.

As they pulled to a halt a second policeman similarly attired, stooped at the driver's window and addressed Katherine.

"Is this you car madam?"

"Yes it is. What's the problem?"

"And the young girl?" asked the policeman peering into the car.

"My niece Lucy."

"And where does she live?" asked the policeman.

"Witchwood."

"Hmm." said the policeman looking at a photograph of Angela on his clipboard and noting the registration number of Katherine's car, "We're looking for a girl, about the same age as your niece, who was abducted from Witchwood three days ago."

"Angela Cummings?" said Katherine.

"She's in my class at school." shouted Lucy from the rear seat of the car.

"I don't suppose you know where she might be?" asked the policeman.

"No but Mr Pemberton will find her." shouted Lucy confidently."

Katherine grimaced.

"Who's this Mr Pemberton?" asked the policeman.

Katherine intervened, "Mr Pemberton lives next door to Lucy but I assure you that he has absolutely nothing to do with the disappearance of Angela Cummings."

"Yes he does," shouted Lucy, "He's going to find her."

"We don't want to get Mr Pemberton into trouble do we, Lucy." said Katherine with a warning glance over her shoulder.

"Right." said the policeman, let's have your full names and addresses and then I'll send someone to have a word with your Mr Pemberton.

Lucy had noticed the warning tone in Katherine's voice and remained silent. The policeman recorded their names and addresses in his notebook then walked over to discuss the matter with his colleague who was busy on his phone checking to see whether Katherine's documents were in order. After casting a few more suspicious glances in their direction, one of the policeman moved a traffic cone and waved them back onto the road.

Lucy waited until the policemen had disappeared into the distance behind them then asked her aunt whether she had got Mr Pemberton into trouble.

"I don't think so Lucy," said Katherine, "but I'd better warn him in case they go banging on his door."

A mile further along the road Katherine stopped the car in a lay-by and telephoned Mr Pemberton to let him know what Lucy had said to the policeman. Mr Pemberton laughed and said that he was pleased that at least someone believed that he could find Angela. He gave Katherine a brief résumé of the limited progress they had made then thanked her for contacting him, wished them a good day then rang off.

Katherine drove on through Henley-in-Arden and Redditch then turned off the Bromsgrove Highway at Batchley and found her way to the car park alongside St Bartholomew's Church in Tardebigge where she stopped the car and turned off the engine.

"Right." said Katherine looking at a map that she had brought with her, "Through the churchyard and down to the canal."

Katherine stopped briefly to look at the church. She had been told that it dated back to Norman times but the church as it stood seemed to her to have all of the characteristics of Georgian architecture. Lucy didn't like churches. She thought they were gloomy places surrounded by graves and made her think of dead people.

The public footpath from the church to the Worcester and Birmingham Canal led down through a large open field in which sheep were quietly grazing. Lupin was put back on his lead.

At the far side of the field a stile led to the canal towpath close to the uppermost of the thirty locks which comprised the Tardebigge flight. When they arrived at the top lock it was not being used so Katherine decided to postpone her explanation of how locks worked until they came to one which was being used. Instead she pointed to the number fifty eight which was displayed on a small cast iron plate fixed to a balancing beam and explained that number allowed the bargee to know which lock he was entering.

From the top lock they followed the towpath towards Worcester. Lupin was let off his lead and scurried about ahead of them investigating anything that caught his attention. They ducked under the brick arched bridge that carried London Lane over the canal and walked on past the old engine house which, Katherine explained, had been built almost two hundred years ago to pump water from the Tardebigge reservoir up to the top lock.

Lucy saw a boat manoeuvring towards the next lock downstream and quickly lost interest in the pumping station. The lock was already full of water and the upper gate had been opened to allow the steersman to guide the boat into the chamber. When the boat was fully inside, two members of the crew closed the gate behind it, wound the paddles closed with a heavy iron turning handle then sprinted to the far end of the lock and wound open the paddles there to let the water out of the chamber. Water began to pour noisily into the canal downstream. This was the part that Lucy liked. She stood as near as she dared to the edge of the chamber and watched the boat sink slowly down between the lock walls. As soon as the water in the lock reached the same level as that of the canal downstream, the two crew members closed the paddles again then put their backs against the two balancing beams and gradually eased the downstream gates open to allow the boat to move down to the third lock in the flight.

Lucy turned to Katherine with a look of sheer joy on her face and asked if she could watch the boat go down in the next lock as well. Lupin liked all of the action and ran about happily.

Lucy watched the same procedure repeated at the next two locks then turned to Katherine and asked how many more locks there were. Katherine did a quick mental calculation and said that there were twenty six more locks in the flight and that it would take the boat another three hours or so to go through them all. Lucy looked as if her interest in locks was beginning to wane so Katherine took the opportunity to lead them up to the top of a bank at the left hand side of the towpath from where they could see Tardebigge reservoir stretched out below them. As they walked along the top of the bank, Lucy could also see the boat they had been watching and at least five of the twenty six locks that it still had to negotiate.

Rather than take Lucy and Lupin back the way they came, Katherine led them across the dam at the far end of the reservoir and through a gate onto a public footpath which ran alongside a ploughed field. Despite the fact that Lucy had been born and brought up in a small village, she was not used to walking in open countryside and held Katherine's hand for reassurance.

"Are there any cows?" asked Lucy who did not like cows because they were big and clumsy and their noses dribbled all the time.

"No Lucy. If you look you will see that the field has been ploughed so that the farmer can plant winter wheat or some other crop. He wouldn't want cows trampling about in his wheat field would he?"

"What sort of field do cows live in then?" asked Lucy.

"They eat grass so they live in a meadow." said Katherine.

Lucy liked her Aunt Katherine because, like Mr Pemberton, she seemed to know everything and took the trouble to explain things to her.

The footpath rose steeply up towards a hedgerow which ran across the top of the field. From there they had a magnificent view across the countryside to the west. Lucy could just pick out a brightly painted narrowboat moving slowly along the canal now well below them. They followed the path through a gap in the hedge and onto a bridleway. Lucy looked at the field which ran alongside the bridleway and could see that it had been ploughed so she didn't have to worry about cows. As they walked along, Lucy and Katherine talked about the trees losing their leaves and about how the birds, rabbits and foxes survived the winter months. Lupin was fascinated by the unfamiliar smells of the countryside and ran about investigating the trails left by the various wild creatures that shared the land with the farmer.

Less than a mile later, the bridleway emerged at the junction of three country roads. Lucy put Lupin back on his lead. Katherine told Lucy to keep Lupin under control and to watch out for drivers who always seemed to be surprised to find pedestrians walking along country roads. They walked in single file back to where the car was parked. The drive home was uneventful and they were back in Witchwood by two o'clock in the afternoon.

The Rubbish Bin

Much earlier that day Mr Wilberforce, with his notebook in his hand, called at Mr Pemberton's house to give him the latest information that he had received from his contact in the police force. Mr Pemberton welcomed him into the house and the two old friends settled themselves down in comfortable armchairs. Mr Wilberforce opened the notebook and began to read.

"Yesterday the caller, just as he had done the previous day, telephoned Mr Cummings at exactly eight o'clock and instructed him to take a notebook and his mobile phone to his car and drive, this time, towards Lapworth. The caller repeated his warning about what would happen if he failed to carry out his instructions then rang off.

"Before he had driven a mile Mr Cummings' phone rang again and the caller told him pull into the side of the road and make a note of six new landmarks. When he'd done that the caller told him to drive around the new route until he rang him again. Just over an hour later, his phone rang and the caller told Mr Cummings to pull into the next lay-by. There, hidden behind a rubbish bin, he would find a mobile phone. He was to leave his own phone in the hiding place, take the other phone with him and continue to drive around the circuit until the replacement phone rang when he was to stop his car and answer it. When he had almost completed the full circuit the phone rang and Mr Cummings pulled his Mercedes to a halt and answered the phone as he had been instructed to do. The caller told Mr Cummings the size of the ransom demand and that it had to be in the form of unmarked, used notes. The full amount had to be available within twenty four hours when he would receive a call on the replacement phone telling him exactly how, when and where he was to deliver it. If the transfer of funds was entirely to the satisfaction of the caller then Angela would be released within the next twenty four hours. Again the caller reminded him of the consequences of failure to do exactly as he was told then rang off.

"Mr Cummings drove home in a rage and told the waiting policemen what had happened then went on to say that he had lost all faith in the ability of the police to arrange the safe release of his daughter and that in future he would handle the matter himself."

With that Mr Wilberforce closed his notebook and looked up at Mr Pemberton who who was obviously deep in thought and several minutes passed before he said anything.

"It's clear," began Mr Pemberton that the kidnappers have deliberately misled the police at every stage. First they sent Mr Cummings to drive for miles through the countryside to give the impression that they could be operating from almost anywhere in central Warwickshire and so managed to persuade the police to extend their search over a huge area. Then they sent Mr Cummings on a different circuit and prevented the police from tracking his phone by the simple expedient of instructing him to leave it in a lay-by then telling him to use a replacement phone that couldn't be tracked. That enabled the kidnappers to provide Mr Cummings with details of the ransom payment knowing that the police would have no record of the conversation that took place and no clue as to the identity or location of the caller. Mr Cummings is now completely disenchanted with the performance of the police force and has refused to cooperate with them. The police are now no closer to finding the kidnappers than they were two days ago."

"And no closer to finding Angela." said Mr Wilberforce despondently.

Both men sat in silence for several minutes then Mr Pemberton suggested that they should try to narrow the field of their enquiry.

Mr Wilberforce was first to speak, "My contact said that the police had traced all of the phone calls made by the kidnappers to Mr Cummings' phone. Apparently all were made from, one or the other, of two different non-android mobile phones and all originated from different points within a mile or so of Witchwood. Does that help?"

"Could the police tell exactly from where each call was made?" asked Pemberton.

"Not exactly." said Mr Wilberforce. "I'm no expert on telephone technology but I understand that the location of a call made from a non-android phone can only be estimated by the triangulation of signal strength received at more than one cell tower and cannot, therefore, be determined with precision. My contact explained that drug dealers and other criminals often use stolen non-android phones of this type in order to avoid detection. He also told me that they rarely made two calls from the same location and sometimes use a stolen phone only once or twice before wiping it clean and throwing it away.

"Perhaps if I were to mark the approximate location of each of the calls on the map," said Mr Wilberforce, "they might at least give us some idea of where the kidnappers operate from."

Mr Pemberton nodded his approval. Mr Wilberforce produced a scale rule and carefully marked each location on the map with a red cross and then added a number to show in what order the calls had been made.

"Even if the locations are only approximate," said Mr Pemberton, "it seems that at least one of the kidnappers is operating much closer to Witchwood than we had thought."

"Or perhaps," said Mr Wilberforce, "the kidnappers are deliberately drawing our attention to Witchwood when Angela is being held miles away."

"Bluff or double bluff," said Mr Pemberton, "We already know that the kidnappers have planned their operation carefully and have done whatever they could to confuse and mislead their pursuers. What we have to decide now is whether the fact that they have made all of their telephone calls from the Witchwood area, is a deliberate ploy to mislead us again, or an indication that the operation is being carried out right under our noses."

"But," said Mr Wilberforce, "even if we were to find that the operation is being coordinated from Witchwood there still remains the possibility that Angela is being held elsewhere. Surely we should concentrate our efforts on finding Angela rather than searching for the kidnappers."

"A very good point Mr Wilberforce." admitted Mr Pemberton, "I was so intrigued by the kidnappers' determination to confuse everybody that I was beginning to forget about Angela."

There was much to be considered. They were beginning to tire, and both men had other matters to attend to, so they decided to adjourn the meeting and meet again at seven o'clock in the evening when they might be able to bring fresh thought to the problem.

The Pile of Prescriptions

Mr Pemberton turned his attention to completing the small pile of prescriptions that had been lying on the mahogany table since they had begun their investigation into Angela's kidnapping. Many of Mr Pemberton's remedies were similar to commercially available medicines but all were carefully prepared by hand from basic ingredients, with measures adjusted to meet individual requirements. Some of his remedies required the infusion of flowers or leaves or the decoction of stems or roots which could take hours to complete. Eventually every prescription was filled and separated into packages each neatly labelled and made ready for delivery. When he had washed all of the equipment that he had used and stored it away, he put on his wellington boots and went to clear some of the autumn leaves that had accumulated in his garden. Lupin, who was playing a noisy game with Lucy in the garden next door, sensed that Mr Pemberton was close by and ran to the fence.

Lucy leapt up onto the millstone, spotted Mr Pemberton at once and shouted, "Hello Mr Pemberton what are you doing?"

Mr Pemberton, as patient as always, pushed a wheelbarrow full of leaves up the fence and leaned over to pat Lupin who he knew would be standing with his paws as far up the fence as he could reach.

"I'm collecting leaves."

"Why?"

"Because the slugs hide under the leaves and eat my cabbages."

Mr Pemberton gathered up armfuls of leaves from the wheelbarrow and put them into a large wire mesh incinerator.

"What are you going to do with the leaves when you've collected them all?" asked Lucy.

"When the wind is blowing away from the houses and no one has any washing out I'll burn them." replied Mr Pemberton.

Mr Pemberton wheeled the barrow back up the garden to collect another load of leaves while Lucy watched in silence.

As Mr Pemberton was consigning the second load of leaves into the incinerator Lucy asked him why the policemen were looking for Angela in Henley-in-Arden.

"I understand that the police are searching for Angela in lots of other places as well." said Mr Pemberton over his shoulder as he set off to collect another load of leaves. Lucy waited until he came back.

"Are you going to find her before the police do?" asked Lucy.

"Mr Wilberforce and I are going to have another meeting later today to see whether we can find out where she is."

"Can I come and listen."

"I'm sorry Lucy," said Mr Pemberton, "but our meeting doesn't take place until after you've gone to bed but we may have something to tell you in the morning."

From Lucy's house came a cry of "Lucy your tea's ready."

"I'd better go or I'll get shouted at." said Lucy, "Goodbye Mr Pemberton I hope the wind blows the right way for you."

Mr Pemberton smiled and returned to collecting leaves. Lucy burst into the kitchen with Lupin at her heals.

"Mr Pemberton's going to have a fire if the wind blows the right way." she explained to her mother.

"Have you washed your hands?" said Mrs Wilson ignoring her explanation about the fire.

"I haven't got them dirty." said Lucy defiantly.

"It doesn't matter Lucy. I've told you hundreds of times that you should never handle food until you have washed your hands."

Lucy pulled a face but wisely decided not to challenge her mother's authority. Instead she made a lot of noise stumping up the stairs to the bathroom. Lupin thought it was a new game and ran after her. Minutes later Lucy was eating her alphabet spaghetti in alphabetical order with each letter balanced on a separate small square of toast. Mrs Wilson shook her head in despair.

When Mr Pemberton heard the distant sound of a bell ringing, he abandoned his leaf clearing operation and went to answer the front door and found two policemen waiting for him in the driveway.

"I imagine," said Mr Pemberton before either of the police officers had uttered a word, "that you are interested in my involvement in the investigation into the kidnapping of Angela Cummings. Come in, sit down and I will explain."

"Thank you sir," said the senior of the two policemen, "That would save time and, as you are no doubt aware, time is in very short supply at the moment."

The two policemen followed him into his living room and, like all new visitors to his house, paused in the doorway to look around.

"Quite a place you've got here." said the sergeant trying to take in some of the detail.

"Yes." said Mr Pemberton, "I'm afraid it's a little untidy at the moment but I can usually find everything that I need.

"Hmm." said the policeman.

"In our spare time I, and my colleague Mr Wilberforce," continued Mr Pemberton, "use the facilities here to investigate any unusual occurrence that is brought to our attention. In view of the fact that Lucy Wilson, who lives next door, is in the same class as Angela Cummings at Witchwood Junior School and regards her a close friend, we chose to investigate the kidnapping."

"And, just as a matter of interest," said the senior officer, "exactly what do your investigations entail?"

"We gather whatever information we can from any source that is available to us and, from that, are trying to puzzle out who the kidnappers are and where Angela is being held. So far we haven't found an answer to either question but I assure you that we will not give up trying until Angela has been found."

"And if you do happen to acquire any useful information?"

"We will of course inform the police force immediately. Here," said Mr Pemberton, passing them a neatly written card, "is the name, rank and telephone number of the officer with whom we have cooperated on many previous occasions."

"We'll check this information of course," said the sergeant, carefully tucking the card into his notebook then getting up from his chair and beckoning his colleague to do the same, "but for the moment it will suffice."

Mr Pemberton escorted the two policemen back to the front door and found Mr Wilberforce ready to press the doorbell.

"This," said Mr Pemberton, "is my colleague Mr Wilberforce."

"Mr Wilberforce," said the senior officer, as he paused to commit Mr Wilberforce's name and face to his memory. "Nice to meet you."

With that the two policeman returned to their car and drove away.

Within a few minutes the two old friends were sitting in comfortable chairs and sharing a pot of tea.

"I've been in touch with my contact in the police force again." began Mr Wilberforce opening his notebook, "In view of the fact that Mr Cummings refuses to cooperate with them, they have looked into his background to see whether they can find anyone with a motive to kidnap his daughter. It turns out that Mr Cummings' involvement in what he refers to as the 'entertainments industry', comprises the ownership of three notorious night clubs in Birmingham and an equally disreputable business supplying gaming machines to various establishments in the West Midlands. It seems that although he does not have a criminal record himself, several of his employees are known to have criminal records ranging from the possession of an illegal weapon to grievous bodily harm. It would appear that Mr Cummings rather than being a respectable family man is, in reality, a ruthless gangster."

"If that is so," said Mr Pemberton, "I imagine there must be a long list of people who have suffered at the hands of Mr Cummings and, no doubt, quite a few who have considered taking their revenge."

"If revenge is the motivation," said Mr Wilberforce, "then what we have assumed to be an elaborate plan simply to deprive a rich man of a large sum of money, might in fact be a carefully devised scheme to deprive him of the only thing that he truly loves, namely his daughter. If the kidnappers are, indeed, motivated by revenge, rather than greed, then they are very much more dangerous individuals than we had thought and Angela's life could be in real danger."

"That settles it," said Mr Pemberton, "We have to forget about finding the kidnappers and concentrate our efforts on finding Angela before she comes to harm."

"But," said Mr Wilberforce, "other than the fact that Angela was somehow abducted quickly and without witnesses, we have very little to work on."

"However limited it is, we can only use the information that we have," said Mr Pemberton. "If no vehicle was seen to enter or leave the new housing development in the few minutes between the time when Angela was last seen and the time that she was reported missing then we have to assume that no vehicle was involved. If no one saw Angela being taken away from the housing development then we have to consider the possibility that she is still being held within it."

"And using the same logic," added Mr Wilberforce, "if no one witnessed a forceful abduction then we must look at the possibility that Angela was not abducted by force but simply persuaded by someone she knew to accompany him, or her, to a secure and soundproof hiding place somewhere within the development."

"Unfortunately," said Mr Pemberton gloomily, "if Angela can identify at least one of the kidnappers then they may already have decided that they cannot afford to leave a living witness behind them when the ransom money has been collected."

"If we believe that Angela's life is in real and immediate danger," said Mr Wilberforce, "then surely we must take our theory, however vague it is, directly to the police."

"If we had any evidence whatsoever to substantiate our theory I would agree with you," said Mr Pemberton with a sigh, "but unfortunately we have none. At present the police are completely overwhelmed by investigations of their own so I doubt that they would be prepared to divert any of their limited resources to investigate a vague hypothesis put forward by two old men."

"Then we will just have to find her

ourselves," said Mr Wilberforce banging his fist on the table, "but how on earth are we to go about it. We have neither the authority nor the resources to enter and search every property within the development and, if we tried to do so without authority, we would almost certainly be arrested before we could find Angela and she would lose what little chance she has of being rescued alive."

"I'm sure you're right Mr Wilberforce," said Mr Pemberton, "so I suggest that we try once again to narrow the field of enquiry.

Mr Wilberforce searched through his collection of maps until he found one which showed the west part of Witchwood in detail. The map showed eighteen large detached houses built adjacent to the two roads that formed a tee shape within the development. An avenue which formed the leg of the tee, ran uphill from the high street to join Hillside which ran across the side of the hill and gave the residents of the largest and most expensive houses in the development an unobstructed view to the south. The Cummings family lived in a five bedroom house towards the west end of Hillside.

They knew that Angela had last been seen turning from the high street into the avenue and from that concluded that Angela may have been seized somewhere within the development. They knew that Angela was not being held captive in the Cummings' house because it had been thoroughly searched by the police. They also knew that Angela's mother, who had been looking out from the house, had not seen her daughter turn from the top of the avenue towards her house in Hillside. From that information alone the two men decided to eliminate from their investigation all six of the houses in the west part of Hillside. Then, because they could think of no reason why Angela should turn right instead of left when she entered Hillside, decided to disregard all of the other houses in that road. The field of enquiry began to narrow.

"If our reasoning is sound," said Mr Pemberton then Angela must be imprisoned in one of the six houses in the avenue."

"It all sounds very convincing," said Mr Wilberforce despairingly, "but surely we are simply adding conjecture to speculation and ending up with little more than guesswork."

"I realise that," admitted Mr Pemberton, "but I can think of no other way to reduce the problem to manageable proportions?"

"Hmm." said Mr Wilberforce.

Mr Pemberton continued, "We know that the police, when they visited every house in the avenue immediately after the abduction, found that only two of the houses in the avenue were occupied. If we assume, or perhaps I should say guess, that it is unlikely that Angela would be held captive in an occupied house then we are left with the problem of how to determine in which of the four unoccupied houses Angela might be held."

"Whatever we do," said Mr Wilberforce, "it is is essential that we do so without attracting too much attention in case we are arrested before can complete the task."

There was long pause while both men considered that aspect of the problem.

Eventually Mr Wilberforce said, "The only way that I can think of to determine in which of the four houses Angela is being held captive, without triggering an alarm system or alerting whoever may be guarding her, is to use Lupin. If we provide him with a sample of Angela's scent we can let him free to search the grounds of each of the four unoccupied houses in turn until he finds her."

"Now we are getting somewhere," said Mr Pemberton triumphantly, "that leaves us only with the problem of what we should do if he finds her."

There was another pause for thought and again Mr Wilberforce was the first to speak, "I suppose if were absolutely sure that Angela was unguarded, we could try to rescue her ourselves but, on reflection, I think the safest course of action would be to tell the police that we have discovered where she is and leave the rescue to them."

By the time they had formulated their plan of action it was far too late in the day to carry it out without drawing attention to themselves so they agreed to meet again at Mr Pemberton's house at seven o'clock in the morning. That would give them time to finalise their plan and make the earliest possible start. Mr Pemberton knew that Mrs Wilson was usually up and about before eight o'clock in the morning so agreed to go next door and discuss the matter with her as soon as he saw or heard any movement in the house. Even if Mrs Wilson at first objected to the idea of using Lupin to help them search for Angela, he felt sure that she would relent when she realised that Angela's life might be in danger if no action was taken.

The Concrete Steps

The next morning, having made a simple breakfast for Mr Wilberforce, Mr Pemberton used the computer to print out an aerial view of the four houses they planned to investigate then studied it for several minutes trying to commit to memory the layout of each of the houses with particular emphasis on rear gardens and any structure which could not be seen from the road. That done he folded up the printout, put it in his pocket and sat down to wait until he saw movement in the house next door. As soon as Mrs Wilson appeared in the kitchen, he went round to the front of her house and rang the bell.

In Lucy's bedroom upstairs Lupin, who had been asleep for hours on his mat by the window, woke up instantaneously, pricked up his ears and listened for movement downstairs. He heard Mrs Wilson's distinctive step as she went to answer the door then heard a muffled voice which, at first, he did not recognise. He moved closer to the bedroom door and listened carefully with his head on one side.

Downstairs Mrs Wilson was surprised to find Mr Pemberton standing in the driveway but invited him in and offered him a cup of tea from the pot she had just made. As usual Mr Pemberton did not refuse the offer of a cup of tea.

Upstairs Lupin recognised Mr Pemberton's voice, put his paw on the door and made a faint grumbling sound. Lucy heard nothing and slept on peacefully.

"I'm sorry to trouble you so early in the morning," began Mr Pemberton, "but Mr Wilberforce and I are now reasonably certain that Angela is being held somewhere in the Hillside development and that her life might be in danger. We would be grateful if you would allow us to use Lupin to determine her exact location so that we can direct the police to rescue her."

Mrs Wilson sat down and considered the matter carefully. She knew that Lupin didn't like to be separated from Lucy so wherever the dog went, so did her daughter. Mr Pemberton waited patiently for her reply. After an interval of several minutes Mrs Wilson asked him whether he knew anything about the people who had kidnapped Angela. Mr Pemberton had to admit that he still did not know who the kidnappers were but that he suspected that at least one of them had crossed swords with Mr Cummings at some time in the past.

"And from what I hear in Witchwood," said Mrs Wilson, "Mr Cummings has some rather unsavoury connections."

"Exactly." said Mr Pemberton. "That's why we need to approach the hiding place with great caution. Our plan is for Mr Wilberforce to park his car in the high street and for Lucy to stay with him while I take Lupin for a stroll up the avenue that leads towards the Cummings' house. I will play the part of a silly old man who allows his little dog to stray into the gardens of neighbouring houses. I will sit on a garden wall or tie my shoelaces to give Lupin time to explore. If I tell him what to look for, it will take him only a matter of minutes to examine each house in turn. As soon as he finds out where she is, I will inform the policemen, who are still on duty outside Mr Cummings' house and leave them to organise her rescue while we sit in the car and await developments."

"With little or no risk to either Lucy or Lupin." said Mrs Wilson with a smile of relief, "I'll have them both fed and ready in less than half an hour."

Upstairs Lupin could sense that something was about to happen and went to wake up Lucy by touching her arm gently with his paw. Lucy stirred luxuriously in the comfort of her bed then yawned, stretched and opened her eyes to see Lupin standing with his paws on the side of the bed. This was unusual behaviour for Lupin who she knew would not normally touch or climb onto the bed. He wagged his tail and did a little dance to show her that something exciting was about to happen. She was already climbing out of bed as her mother knocked and entered the bedroom.

"Mr Pemberton has been round to say that if you can eat your breakfast, wash and dress in less than half an hour you and Lupin can help him to find Angela."

Lucy needed no persuasion. She ran downstairs, gobbled her breakfast, drank her fruit juice and ran back upstairs to wash, clean her teeth and dress in outdoor clothes and was waiting excitedly for Mr Pemberton within less than twenty minutes. Mrs Wilson had never seen her move so quickly and just had time to check her over, tidy her hair and pull her socks up to the same level, when Mr Pemberton rang the front door bell again. Mrs Wilson answered the door and Lucy dragged him into the house while Lupin ran around enthusiastically.

"Have you found Angela yet?" asked Lucy.

"Not yet," replied Mr Pemberton, "but we think we know in which part of Witchwood she is being held prisoner and need Lupin to tell us exactly where she is."

"He'll find her." said Lucy confidently, "he's a clever little dog."

"First we need something of Angela's so

that Lupin can recognise her scent." said Mr Pemberton

"What sort of thing?" asked Lucy

"Preferably something made of cotton or wool that will hold Angela's scent." answered Mr Pemberton.

Lucy thought silently for a moment then said doubtfully, "All I've got is Angela's crocodile which I swapped for my gorilla last week. Will that do?"

When Mr Pemberton looked baffled, Mrs Wilson intervened to explain that both the crocodile and the gorilla were monster finger dolls.

Mr Pemberton turned to Lucy and asked her whether she could show him the doll. Lucy ran upstairs and reappeared a few seconds later with a small puppet, in the shape of a crocodile, fitted onto her finger and moved it about making a hissing sound to represent the sort of sound that she imagined a crocodile might make. Mr Pemberton asked Mrs Wilson whether she would allow Lupin to put his front paws on the low table. Normally Lupin would have been scolded for doing anything like that in the Wilson household but on this occasion Mrs Wilson made an exception. Lupin was reluctant to follow Mr Pemberton's instructions until Mrs Wilson tapped the table with her hand to show that she approved.

When Lupin was standing with his paws on the table, Mr Pemberton bent forward in his chair and looked into his eyes. Lucy had seen them do this on several occasions and was not at all surprised to see them do it again. Mrs Wilson watched with a slightly puzzled expression. Mr Pemberton told Lucy to place the finger doll on the table in front of Lupin then to stand back. Lupin lowered his head and sniffed the doll then looked up at Mr Pemberton. For a minute there seemed to be some sort of silent communication between man and dog then Lupin stepped down from the low table and went to sit by Lucy.

"It's not as strange as it looks'" said Mr Pemberton to Mrs Wilson, "Lupin knows that when I ask him to stand in that way, I intend to give him an instruction. When he sniffed the doll he easily separated Angela's scent from Lucy's and remembered that he had met Angela before on several occasions. He now knows that he is looking for Angela and all I have to do is point him in the right direction."

Mrs Wilson still looked doubtful but said nothing.

"Now with your permission I think it's time that we began our search for Angela." said Mr Pemberton.

In Mr Wilberforce's little blue car they drove down to the high street and parked close to the avenue. Mr Pemberton climbed out of the car and raised the front passenger seat so that Lupin could join him. Immediately Lupin took an interest in the pavement along the high street but did not seem able to separate Angela's scent trail from the confusion of the other trails. Mr Pemberton led him around the corner into the avenue where Lupin found more clearly defined trails to follow. He assumed his usual zigzag search pattern so that he missed nothing. He looked up at Mr Pemberton and wagged his tail and ran from side to side to show that Angela had followed several slightly different routes on her way home. He paused near one property where the scent was particularly strong. That suggested to Mr Pemberton that Angela may have stopped at that point to talk to someone.

The trail grew stronger as they turned from the avenue into Hillside. From there Lupin crossed the road diagonally, trotted past two policemen who were standing guard, put his head between the bars of the large wrought iron front gates of the Cummings' residence and wagged his tail furiously. Mr Pemberton realised that Lupin was indicating the trail of the strongest scent trail and for a moment wondered whether it was possible that Angela was hiding or being held captive in her own house. Whatever the case he realised that the young dog had done exactly what he had been instructed to do so he bent down to make a fuss of him.

One of the policemen asked Mr Pemberton why the little dog had taken such an interest in the driveway to the Cummings' house. Pemberton told him that Lupin was one of the finest tracker dogs he had ever worked with and that they were trying to track Angela's last known movements in the hope that they might find her.

"Well you won't find her in there," said the policeman indicating the Cummings' abode, "we searched it from top to bottom yesterday."

Mr Pemberton knew that the police, in the case of abduction, always made a thorough search of the victim's home. Frequently they found the victim imprisoned in, or sometimes simply hiding in, their own house. Occasionally they found indications that a more brutal crime had taken place and turned their attention to searching for a body.

A change of approach was required. Mr Pemberton led Lupin back into the avenue and asked him to search the grounds of each of the four unoccupied houses in turn. At the first house Mr Pemberton simply opened the front gate and allowed Lupin into the garden. Lupin zigzagged his way along the drive up the front of the house then squeezed under a gate that led to the rear garden and disappeared from sight. Two minutes later he returned and showed no sign of having picked up Angela's scent. At the second house Mr Pemberton had to lift Lupin over the front wall. Lupin carried out a similar search then returned without having found her.

The third house that they examined was a large white detached house separated from the road by a low brick built boundary wall and an immaculately manicured lawn and carefully tended flower beds. From a pair of wrought iron gates near the left hand end of the front boundary wall, a gravel driveway led to a double garage adjacent to the house. At the right hand end of the wall was a single gate marked 'Tradesman's Entrance". It was near this gateway that Lupin had hesitated when they had first walked up the avenue.

Mr Pemberton opened the gate quietly and Lupin followed a scent trail along a narrow gravel path that ran at the side of the lawn towards a wooden gate which gave access to the rear garden. The gate was slightly ajar so Lupin nudged it open and disappeared behind the house. It was several minutes before he emerged from the gate and ran towards Mr Pemberton wagging his tail triumphantly as he performed a spectacular waggle dance to show that he had found where Angela was being held. Mr Pemberton made a fuss of him then took the aerial photograph from his pocket and examined the garden at the rear of the house. There appeared to be no shed or other structure in the garden in which a prisoner could be securely held, but when he looked more closely at the rear of the house itself, he saw a short flight of concrete steps leading down to what he suspected was the door of a basement. He was then almost certain that he now knew exactly where Angela was being kept.

First he walked back to the car and told the other two what Lupin had found. Lucy whooped with joy and made an enormous fuss of Lupin. Then they drove up the avenue and parked near to the two policemen who were standing guard outside Mr Cummings' house. Mr Pemberton eased himself out of the small car again and approached them.

"Back again sir," said the policemen to whom he had spoken to earlier, "how can we help you this time?"

"I thought you would like to know," began Mr Pemberton with a pleasant smile, "that we believe that we have discovered where Angela Cummings is being held prisoner."

The policeman looked at his colleague who shrugged his shoulders non-committally.

"And what makes you think that sir?"

asked the first policeman with just the merest hint of sarcasm.

"Because the little dog, that you saw earlier, tracked Angela to the place where she is now being held prisoner." said Mr Pemberton calmly.

"Hmm," said the policeman, "And where exactly do you believe that she is being held?"

"In the rear basement of No.5 The Avenue which is, as you may know, less than two hundred yards from where we are standing."

"And your name sir?" asked the policeman reaching for his pocket book.

"Albert Pemberton. And here" said Mr Pemberton as he handed the policeman a small piece of paper, "is the name, rank and telephone number of our contact in the police force with whom we have worked on several previous occasions and, I am sure, will vouch for us."

The policeman copied the information into his pocketbook, reached for his phone and asked to speak to the officer coordinating the Cummings enquiry. There was a short pause while the call was transferred then the policeman gave his name and location before relaying, almost word for word, everything that Mr Pemberton told him. There was another pause while he listened to the reply then added the name and telephone number of Mr Pemberton's contact in the police force. This time there was a longer delay while information was checked and a decision made.

Eventually a reply came and the policeman responded, "Yes sir. Yes. Right. About fifteen minutes. Yes sir. OK.

He clipped his phone back onto his uniform and, still looking suspiciously at Mr Pemberton, said, "The coordinator says that, in view of the fact that there may be some dangerous characters involved in the kidnapping, they're going to send an armed response unit to investigate the matter. It should be here in about fifteen minutes. You are to stay where you are and wait until the ARU arrives."

While they were waiting Mr Pemberton explained to the policeman that the little girl, who was talking excitedly to his colleague Mr Wilberforce in the car, was a close friend of Angela Cummings. The policeman asked for the names and addresses of all of the occupants of the car and entered them into his pocketbook.

Ten minutes later an unmarked black van with darkened windows drove quietly up the avenue, turned into Hillside and parked where it could not be seen from the avenue. The side door of the van slid open silently and eight fully armed policemen wearing black overalls, helmets and goggles, slipped noiselessly out of the van and sheltered in a line against a nearby wall while they waited for instructions. The team leader walked over to the two policemen and told them that there was now an ambulance and another armed police unit waiting at the far end of the avenue, then asked them whether there had been any activity at No.5 since they had called for assistance. The policemen told him that they had seen no activity at all. The team leader asked whether he knew for certain, or simply suspected, that the girl was being held captive at No.5. At that point Mr Pemberton introduced himself and explained that his tracker dog had given him a positive indication that Angela was being held, possibly in a basement, at the rear of the house. Mr Pemberton added that, in view of the possibility that she might have been guarded, he had decided not to investigate the property himself. The team leader nodded his approval then asked him why, if he hadn't investigated the rear of the house, he thought that Angela was being held in a basement. Mr Pemberton took the aerial photograph from his pocket and showed him where Lupin had found his way to the rear of the house then showed him the steps which he suspected led down from the rear garden to a basement of some sort. He also pointed out that there did not appear to be any other structure at the rear of the house which could be used to hold someone captive. The leader studied the photograph then asked him whether he had seen or heard anyone in, or near, the property when he was there. Mr Pemberton said that he had not. The leader asked whether he could keep the photograph and Mr Pemberton agreed.

The team leader said nothing for a few seconds while he considered his plan of attack then said, "Right. We'll go in at the right hand side of the house leaving two men to secure the front elevation. We'll enter the basement first and if the girl is not there we'll enter and search the rest of the house and grounds."

With that he rejoined his men, told them his plan and led them in single file around the corner into the avenue. Less than a minute after the armed response unit had disappeared from view, Mr Pemberton and the two policemen heard three loud bangs then muffled cries as the armed response unit went into action. Then silence.

Mr Pemberton and the two policemen moved to a position at the top of the avenue from which they could see the house that was being raided. At first they could see only two members of the response unit crouching motionless in the front garden then suddenly a third member of the team emerged from the gate at the side of the house carrying a bundle in his arms. When he was safely in the avenue he knelt down allowed the small and obviously terrified figure of a young girl to stagger to her feet. The ambulance arrived within seconds and medical staff leapt out to attend to the girl. Seconds later with screams of 'armed police, armed police' members of the response unit broke into the house and searched it from bottom to top but found no one. A number of policemen arrived from the far end of the avenue and began to cordon off the house with blue and white tape in order to seal the site for forensic examination. Then the two policemen that Mr Pemberton had been talking to, ran down the avenue to offer their assistance but were sent back straight away to give the good news to Mrs Cummings and to escort her to the ambulance in which Angela was now being made comfortable. Mr Pemberton walked back to the car and told his colleagues that Angela had been released and seemed to be unharmed. Lucy whooped with joy and gave Lupin a hug that made him squeak. Mr Pemberton climbed back into the car and shook hands with Mr Wilberforce.

The cordon that the police had established at the junction with the high street was lifted to allow waiting reporters and television cameramen to flood into the avenue. No one paid much attention to the little blue car as it nosed its way slowly homewards through the gathering crowd of onlookers.

The Gardener

As soon as they returned to Mr Pemberton's house, Mr Wilberforce went in to update his records on the computer while Mr Pemberton escorted Lucy and Lupin back to their own house. Mrs Wilson had been watching out for them and answered the door before Mr Pemberton could ring the bell.

Lucy rushed through the door shouting, "Mum, mum, Lupin found Angela behind a house and she's alright but they've put her in an ambulance and there are lots of people all over the place."

Mrs Wilson looked at Mr Pemberton for confirmation.

"Lucy's jumbled it up bit of course," said Mr Pemberton with a smile, "but she's right. Lupin did follow Angela's scent to the basement of a house in the avenue. The police organised a raid by an armed response unit and Angela was released, obviously distressed but apparently unharmed."

"And we stopped outside Angela's house which is very big and has railings all round it and the black policemen had guns but I don't think they shot anybody" shouted Lucy as she ran off to help Lupin who seemed to have lost something under the settee.

"Do the police know who the kidnappers are yet?" asked Mrs Wilson.

"I'm almost certain," replied Mr Pemberton, "that Angela spoke, on more than one occasion, to the man who kidnapped her but, of course, the police will not be able to confirm that until she has been given a thorough medical examination.

"Who do *you* think the kidnappers are?" asked Mrs Wilson.

"Well," said Mr Pemberton with a sigh, "I, like everyone else involved in this affair have been misled on several occasions during the last few days but I now believe that the man who spoke to Mr Cummings and gave the impression that he was the spokesman for an organised gang of kidnappers was, in reality, working alone and devised an elaborate plan to lead his pursuers astray. I think that he came to Witchwood with the sole purpose of seeking revenge against Mr Cummings for some unforgivable deed in the past and, in order to get closer to the Cummings' house, decided to masquerade as a gardener at one of the unoccupied houses in the avenue. I suspect that he planned to gain Angela's confidence by holding short friendly conversations with her as she passed by him on her way to and from school then, one day, when she stopped to admire the garden, somehow, perhaps by telling her that there was an even more beautiful garden behind the house, managed to spirit her away without a sound. The rest you know."

"Of course," continued Mr Pemberton, "now that the kidnapper has left his victim alive, he is himself in grave danger. Unless the police find him before Mr Cummings does, I think we may find ourselves investigating a brutal murder in the not too distant future."

Mrs Wilson didn't appreciate Mr Pemberton's curious sense of humour, but thanked him for taking the trouble to explain what had happened in such detail.

"All that's left for me to do now," said Mr Pemberton, "is to thank all three of you for your assistance. Had it not been for your help I think that Angela might not have survived."

"Now," continued Mr Pemberton, "I'm sure that Lucy has much to tell you so, if you will forgive me, I will go home to help Mr Wilberforce to complete his report."

Mrs Wilson escorted him to the door and thanked him again for keeping Lucy out of harm's way. As the door closed, Mrs Wilson turned to find Lucy running towards her shouting, "Where's he gone I wanted to talk to him?"

Other books in the series:

1.   Lucy and Lupin and the Terrorists.

2.   Lucy and Lupin and the Drug Dealers.

3.   Lucy and Lupin and the Smugglers.

4.   Lucy and Lupin and the Bank Robbers.

5.   Lucy and Lupin and the Aeroplane.

6.   Lucy and Lupin and the Basket of Puppies.

7.   Lucy and Lupin and the Kidnappers.

8.   Lucy and Lupin and the White Van.

9.   Lucy and Lupin and the Silver Chalice.